KATIE HICKS

FLYING EYE BOOKS

BATTLING...
6:50
...DAY IN, DAY OUT...
...WITH NO END IN SIGHT.
WITH ONLY AN ELIXIR FOR STRENGTH BY MY SIDE...
...AND MY NERVE...
...WHICH HAS BEEN WANING.

BUT TONIGHT I AM POWERFUL.
HP
WINNING AND...
...LOSING.
LOTS OF LOSING.

BUT TODAY WILL BE MY DAY.
MY DAY TO THRIVE.
MORE POWERFUL—
BZZZ
BZZZ
BZZZ
GOOD MORNING, GALE!
IT'S 7:00AM ALREADY?!
BZZZ
BZZZ

QUIET! QUIET! QUIET!
REMINDER!
MOM'S BIRTHDAY TOMORROW!
REMINDER!
ASSIGNMENT DUE!
LATE FOR CLASS!
CLASS IN 30 MINS!
DON'T BE LATE!
BZZZ
BZZZ
REMINDER!
CALL GRANDMA!

ALRIGHT, ALRIGHT, ALRIGHT! I GET IT!
SNOOZE 30 SECS?
YES
I'M GOING TO BE LATE FOR CLASS!
IT'S GOOD, IT'S FINE, I'M HANDING IT IN ON TIME AND EVERYTHING.
REMINDER!
HAVE A CALMING SIMPLY PEAR BEVERAGE TO START YOUR DAY OFF RIGHT!
RIGHT!

BE LATE AGAIN!
DENTIST!
OKAY, HERE WE GO. TIME TO START A RELAXING, PRODUCTIVE, AND ENJOYABLE DAY.
SLAM
I CAN DO THIS.
I CAN DO THIS.
I CAN DO THIS.
WITH SIMPLY PEAR™ PRODUCTS, YOU CAN ACCOMPLISH ANYTHING!
BZZZ
I CAN DO THIS.
I CAN DO THIS...
BZZZ
BZZZ

I'VE... GOT THIS...
ASSIGNMENT DUE!
GO TO CLASS!
DON'T BE LATE!
ALRIGHTY.
HONK!!
BEEP BEEP!!
HONK HONK!!
BEEP!
HONK!
I CAN DO IT... I CAN GO TO CLASS. IT'S JUST HANDING IN AN ASSIGNMENT.
HERE AT SIMPLY PEAR...

SIMPLY PEAR!

SO SIMPLE... :)

NEW!

WE BELIEVE THAT WELL-BEING STARTS WITH TACKLING THE ANXIETY AND NEGATIVITY THAT DRAGS US DOWN.

PEAR MADE SIMPLE

WE'VE MADE IT OUR MISSION TO HELP, AND WITH ALL-NATURAL PRODUCTS, WE HAVE THE ANSWER!

12 VERIFIED BETA-D COMPOUNDS!
6 DUAL-EXTRACTED B+ VITAMINS!
1 EASY SOLUTION!
ALL IN OUR SIMPLE 57-PRODUCT LINE! YOU'LL BE SOARING ABOVE STRESS AND ANXIETY IN NO TIME!
BZZZ
SIMPLE
AND WITH OUR NEW APP, YOU'LL GET PERSONALIZED ADVICE ON THE GO!
THINGS WILL BE FINE!
THINGS WILL BE FINE!
BZZZ!!
YOU'RE LATE!

OKAY!

I CAN DO THIS.

CLASS! I NEED YOU ALL TO LISTEN UP!
SQUEAK

YOUR PROJECTS ARE DUE BUT WE'LL BE DOING SOMETHING A LITTLE DIFFERENT TODAY.
CRIT
FOR THIS ASSIGNMENT WE'LL BE...
SCREETCH
...PRESENTING OUR WORK TO OUR PEERS...
...IN FRONT OF THE CLASS!
UGH
ANY VOLUNTEERS TO GO FIRST?
I'LL GO!
OKAY, OKAY, STAY CALM.

AHEM.
MY PROJECT TODAY EXPLORES THE TRUE BEAUTY OF FREEDOM AND CONNECTION IN THE 21ST CENTURY.
CLAP CLAP
EXCELLENT WORK!
THIS PIECE MEANS A LOT TO ME. I REALLY PUT MY HEART AND SOUL ON THIS CANVAS.
OH NO, OH NO, OH NO...
I THOUGHT WE WERE JUST HANDING THEM IN!
CLACK CLACK
BZZZ
BZZZ
REMEMBER TO GET OUT OF YOUR COMFORT ZONE AND EMBRACE LIFE!

I CAN'T, I CAN'T!
AMAZING WORK, WHO'S NEXT?

PUT 100% IN EVERY DAY!

ANYONE?

COME ON, FOLKS! THIS IS A GREAT WAY TO ENGAGE WITH EACH OTHER'S WORK.
REALLY? NO ONE?
EVERY DAY YOU ARE GETTING STRONGER! NOW SHOW THE WORLD!

SCHOOL IS MEANT TO BE FUN!
RUNNING AWAY FROM EVERYTHING IS COUNTERPRODUCTIVE!
YOU WON'T ACCOMPLISH ANYTHING WITH THAT ATTITUDE!
SLAM
SLAM
PANT PANT PANT

I'LL *HUFF* HAND IT IN LATER, *HUFF* AT LEAST I *HUFF* WENT TO SCHOOL...
THUD

PERSONALIZED ADVICE...
HERE TO HELP!! :)

YOU'RE AMAZING!
AHH!!
I GUESS THAT COULD BE USEFUL.

ANY ADVICE TO NOT HUMILIATE MYSELF FURTHER WOULD BE GREEEAT.
THUD

I NEED TO LIE DOWN!

GO IN THERE AND MAKE A GOOD IMPRESSION! UNLIKE THE LAST ROOMMATE YOU NEVER TALKED TO!

BZZZ

OKAY...

I CAN DO THIS.

I'M NOT DOING IT!

COME ON, WHY NOT?

JOB HUNTING IS NOT MY IDEA OF A "COOL FUN TIME."

YOU CAN BE MY HYPE MAN!

FOR THE LAST TIME, NO!

JUST A LITTLE BIT FARTHER...

IS THIS A BREAK AND ENTRY?

I UH... LIVE HERE...

AWESOME!
I'M NOT SUPER EQUIPPED TO DEAL WITH A BURGLARY SITUATION!

MY NEW ROOMMATE'S HERE!
THAT'S GREAT. YOU'RE STILL NOT LEAVING ALL THE UNPACKING TO ME.
I'M AIDEN AND I SWEAR I'M A SUPER GOOD ROOMMATE.
OKAY...

THAT'S NOT CONVINCING AT ALL.

THAT'S MASON. HE WON'T BE INVITED OVER VERY OFTEN.

THUMP

AND YOU ARE..?

OH. I'M G-GALE...

IS THAT A WIZARD?

AND I DON'T SAY THAT TO JUST ANYBODY.

DO WE GO TO THE SAME SCHOOL? I HAVEN'T SEEN YOU AROUND?

UHH... WE MUST JUST BE MISSING EACH OTHER...

WE SHOULD HANG OUT SOMETIME! DO SOME ROOMMATE BONDING—I'M FREE ALL TOMORROW?

WHAT HAPPENED TO YOUR SUPER COOL JOB SEARCH?

WE CAN GO EARLY!
I... I DON'T KNOW...
I'LL PENCIL YOU IN FOR FIRST THING TOMORROW MORNING, THEN!
I'M, UH, PRETTY SW—
JIGGLE
JIGGLE
SWAMPED!
UH...
SICKNESS... I HAVE SWAMP SICKNESS.
OH! THAT SOUNDS REALLY SERIOUS!

I'M GOING TO LIE DOWN.

OKAY!

WE CAN HANG OUT ANOTHER TIME.

YEAH, FOR SURE.

CLICK

BZZZ

DITCHING SCHOOL NOW DITCHING NEW FRIENDS? THAT'S NO WAY TO BUILD A HAPPY FUTURE! :)

UGGHHHHHH
DON'T FORGET TO DRINK YOUR SIMPLY PEAR DAILY!
BZZ

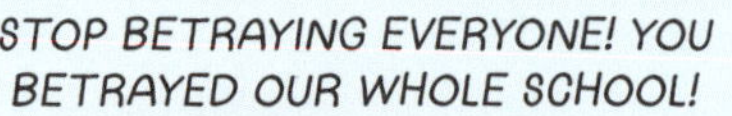

I HATE YOU.

I HATE YOU!

I DON'T PAINT WITH MY HANDS, I PAINT WITH MY SOUL.

ACHIEVE WITHOUT FEAR!

THE ONLY WAY IS TO SHOW UP EVERY DAY.

EAT. SLEEP. BREATHE. PAINT.

MY 5AM RUNS FUEL MY LIFE AND MY CREATIVE SPIRIT.

I LOVE BEING FEARLESS AND WELL-ADJUSTED!
OH, COME ON.
NOW FROM OUR SPONSOR, SIMPLY PEAR!

Hmm...

OVERDUE AND UNDERWHELMING!
ITS COOL AND ALL, BUT I REALLY WISH YOU HADN'T LIED TO ME. WHAT EVEN IS SWAMP SICKNESS?

WHAT'S EVEN THE POINT? I'M STAYING IN THIS ROOM FROM HERE ON OUT!

STUPID SCHOOL.
STUPID EVERYONE, HAVING IT SO EASY.
I GIVE UP.
I'M DESTINED TO BE AN OLD MAN THAT LIVES IN THE MOUNTAINS AND DOESN'T TALK TO ANYONE...
I KNOW IT!
BZZZ
HMM...
NEW UPDATE!!
HERE AT SIMPLY PEAR, WE CARE!
THE PAIN AND ANXIETY YOU FEEL DAY IN, DAY OUT CAN BE ERASED!
BE BRAVE!
!!!!
CONNECT WITH OTHERS!
EAT A PEAR!
DON'T YOU WANT TO BE FREE FROM THE PAIN AND UNCOMFORTABLENESS OF LIFE?

IT CAN BE AS SIMPLE AS TRYING A FEW EASY-TO-USE PRODUCTS!
AND YOU'LL BE SOARING IN NO TIME!

CONNECT WITH OTHERS AND BE OPEN TO NEW EXPERIENCES!
BZZZ BZZZ BZZZ

ANYTHING LESS IS FAILURE!

SIGH

TOSS
IT'S A LOST CAUSE. I'M MOVING TO THE MOUNTAINS.

TRY YOUR BEST ALL DAY, EVERY DAY!

BZZZ!!
BZZZ!!
BZZZ!!
BZZZ!!

MOUNTAIN LIFE DOESN'T SEEM TOO BAD.
RAISE SOME GOATS, MAYBE A HORSE?
BZZZ
BZZZ
BZZZ
BZZZ

BZZZ
BZZZ

BEING YOU EVERY DAY MUST BE PAINFUL.
YOU STRUGGLE TO GO TO CLASS.
YOU STRUGGLE TO MAKE FRIENDS.
YOU STRUGGLE WITH EVERYTHING!
PRONE TO EMBARRASSMENT!
PAINFULLY AWKWARD.

EVERY DAY, A NEW HUMILIATION!
REMEMBER WHEN YOU WERE TWELVE AND YOU WERE TOO SCARED TO GO TO THE SCHOOL DANCE?
HAHA HAHA HAHA
SO YOU LIT YOUR SHOES ON FIRE AS A DESPERATE ATTEMPT TO GET OUT OF GOING?
NEW!! NEW!! NEW!!
GALE?
OR WHEN YOU FORGOT YOUR PAINTS IN CLASS AND YOU WERE TOO SCARED TO ASK TO BORROW ANY SO YOU JUST MIMED PAINTING FOR THREE HOURS?
OR HOW YOU'VE MISSED TWELVE DAYS OF THIS SEMESTER JUST BECAUSE YOU'RE SCARED PEOPLE WILL LAUGH AT YOUR ART?

JUST TODAY, YOU BAILED ON CLASS AGAIN AND LIED TO A POTENTIAL FRIEND!
A WHOLE LIFE OF AVOIDANCE, GALE!
A WHOLE LIFE!
A WHOLE LIFE!
IS THIS HOW YOUR WHOLE LIFE IS GOING TO BE, GALE? RUNNING AT THE FIRST SIGN OF FEAR?

ALL YOU HAVE IS FEAR!
FEAR!
FEAR!
RUNNING AWAY AGAIN, GALE?
WHEN ARE YOU GOING TO STOP RUNNING AWAY?
GALE...
GALE...
GALE!
GALE!!!

YOU GOOD?
"CRUNCH"
"CRUNCH"
"HUFF"
"HUFF"
TOMORROW! OUT! I'LL HANG OUT WITH YOU TOMORROW!
WOW! SWAMP SICKNESS PASSES FAST!
YOU'RE LOOKING BETTER ALREADY! DOES 1PM WORK? I DON'T WANT TO WAKE UP BEFORE NOON.
HUFF
HUFF
HUFF 1PM *HUFF* WORKS...

AWESOME!
WE'LL BE HITTING THE TOWN SO HARD, THEY WON'T EVEN KNOW WHAT HIT THEM! COOL?
COOL.
THUD!!
THAT'S THE SPIRIT!
CLAP!!
HERE AT SIMPLY PEAR, WE WANT YOU TO BELIEVE IN YOURSELF. WE KNOW WE'RE THE BEST WAY FOR YOU TO DO JUST THAT!

IT'LL BE FINE.
YOU CAN DO THIS.
IT'LL BE OVER BEFORE YOU KNOW IT.

LET'S GO,
LET'S GO!
AFTER YOU!
THANKS...
GRAB A SEAT
NEAR THE BACK!
PRINCESS CANNON
KNIFE STICKER? IS THAT
YOUR SKETCHBOOK?
CAN I LOOK
THROUGH IT?
S-SURE, IF YOU WANT.

WOW!
THESE ARE AMAZING!
YOU'RE A TRUE ARTISTE.
I WOULDN'T SAY THAT...
OF COURSE! THIS WOULD BE PERFECT FOR A BAND POSTER!
WAIT! YOU SHOULD DESIGN A POSTER FOR MY BAND!
YOU HAVE A BAND?
OF COURSE I DO, I'M SUPER COOL.

SIMPLE
I'LL SEND YOU A VISION BOARD LATER.
BUT I'VE NEVER DONE A BAND POSTER!
WITH ART LIKE THIS, I'M NOT WORRIED.
OH! THIS LOOKS LIKE OUR STOP!
PULL

OKAY, JUST ONE QUICK STOP. THEN DRINKS ON ME!
I'VE GOT TO HAND OUT SOME OF THESE BAD BOYS.
THANKS!
RÉSUMÉ
A+!
GREAT!
WHY DON'T YOU JUST APPLY ONLINE?
OH, MY DAD SAYS THAT'S A BUNCH OF TECHNO GARBAGE. GOTTA HIT THE PAVEMENT RUNNING.
BESIDES, I DON'T HAVE A COMPUTER. COMPLETELY BRICKED. FELL OFF A ROOF.
THUD
?
ALRIGHT, LET'S GO!

DING
ICE. TIME.
FREEZE ZONE!!
STAFF ONLY
!!
REJUVINATING PEAR PUREE
SIMPLE.

ALRIGHTY, NOW TO TURN ON THE CHARM.
GOOD DAY, MONSIEUR.
WELCOME TO SLUSHIE GALAXY WHERE THE ICE IS OUTTA THIS W—
YOU'RE NOT GETTING ANY MORE FREE DRINKS.
OH, I INTEND TO PAY FOR THOSE DRINKS AND...
I'D LIKE TO SPEAK TO THE MANAGER.
REUSME
RÉSUMÉ
•Fun loving!
•Great smile →
AIDEN
Always on time!
Interested in work!
Don't not hire me!
Excellent @ everything!
NOT A BAD EMPLOYEE!
I AM THE MANAGER.
AIDEN, NO. ITS NOT HAPPENING.
Stick
COME ON, WHY NOT?

YOU STEAL FROM HERE CONSTANTLY! YOU CAN'T OPEN A TAB AT A SLUSHIE PLACE
AND EVEN IF YOU COULD, YOU STILL HAVE TO PAY IT!
SPEAKING OF PAYING, LET'S SEE HOW MUCH YOU OWE...
OH, YOU DON'T HAVE TO DO THAT...
FINE. I'LL PAY WHEN I GET THE JOB!
YOU'RE NOT GETTING A JOB HERE!
HOW DID YOU GET ROPED INTO THIS?
UH... EMOTIONAL SUPPORT?
REFRESHING PEAR!!
CALMING PEAR!!
I REALLY DON'T HAVE TIME. I'M TRYING TO FIGURE OUT WHAT'S HAPPENING WITH WEDNESDAY'S SHOW.
DRIP DRIP DRIP
ON COMPANY TIME..?
MIA'S SAID SHE'S ROPED IN SOME DODGEBALL LEAGUE TO COME, BUT WE STILL NEED SOME NON-DODGEBALLERS TO LEVEL OUT THE CROWD.
I'M WORRIED THEY'RE GONNA START THROWING THINGS.
SMILE!

WELL, IT LOOKS LIKE I'M HERE TO SAVE THE DAY. MY LOVELY NEW FRIEND WITH HIS MILD-MANNERED TEMPERAMENT WILL MELLOW OUT THE DODGEBALLERS!
W-WHAT DO YOU MEAN?
ASTRAL PANIC! THE BAND I TOLD YOU ABOUT, WE'RE PLAYING THIS WEDNESDAY!
WE'RE AMAZING. THIS IS OUR FIRST SHOW WITH AN AUDIENCE!

A BIG, HUGE CROWD OF DODGEBALLERS. AND GALE!
SOUNDS LIKE A NIGHTMARE.
HAHA!
DODGEBALLERS AND GALE! DODGEBALLERS AND GALE!
TAKE THAT, NERD!
HA
HA
HA
NO!
HA
HA
HA
HA
GET HIM!
HA
HA
GET BACK HERE!
SO, WHAT DO YOU THINK?

I UH... UH... UH...
UM...
I CAN'T. I CAN'T DO THAT... I UH, HAVE AN ASSIGNMENT DUE THAT NIGHT.
OH, CLASS AT NIGHT?
MHM, NIGHT CLASS...
THAT'S FINE. WE'LL FIGURE SOMETHING ELSE OUT.
I'LL WRANGLE UP A CROWD, DON'T YOU WORRY ABOUT IT!
I'M TEXTING HARPER.
LET'S SEE IF SHE HAS ANY IDEAS.
THANKS!
MASON, PUT THIS ON MY TAB. I'VE GOT A BIG DAY AHEAD OF ME AND PLACES TO BE.
BZZZ

BENDING TO FEAR ONCE AGAIN? WE ALL HAVE OUR FAIR SHARE OF FAILURES! :)
DING
Hm...
I HAVE A COUPLE MORE PLACES TO HIT UP TODAY. I WAS REALLY HOPING HE'D JUST GIVE ME THE JOB.

AND IF THE SHOW TURNS OUT TO BE A FAILURE, WHATEVER! I JUST NEED TO FOCUS ON THE JOB HUNT!
BZZZ
LEAVING A POTENTIAL FRIEND HIGH AND DRY? REMEMBER TO ALWAYS BE THERE FOR OTHERS!
FAILURE!
FAILURE!
UH, I...
UH... YOU OKAY?

I'M... I...
ARE YOU FEELING SICK AGAIN?
I'M... I'M...
EXHAUSTED!
ALL I'VE BEEN EATING IS SIMPLY PEAR PRODUCTS FOR WEEKS!
!
MY PHONE KEEPS REMINDING ME OF ALL MY FAILURES!
I'M TRYING SO HARD TO JUST BE BRAVE AND FUNCTION PROPERLY, BUT I FEEL WORSE THAN EVER!

SIMPLY PEAR!

SIMPLY PEAR? I THINK I'VE SEEN THAT STUFF AROUND, EVERYONE ONLINE WON'T STOP TALKING ABOUT IT.

IT'S SUPPOSED TO HELP *HUFF* *HUFF* WITH CONFIDENCE!

SORRY, I'M A TERRIBLE PERSON TO HANG OUT WITH. I SHOULDN'T HAVE EVEN COME ALONG.
WELL, IF YOU WANT TO GET OUT MORE, I'M DROPPING OFF RÉSUMÉS ALL DAY.

I'VE BEEN TOLD I HAVE A DANGEROUS AMOUNT OF CONFIDENCE.
I CAN BESTOW UPON YOU MY KNOWLEDGE, AND IN TURN YOU CAN BE MY HYPE MAN!
HYPE... MAN?
COME ON! IT'LL BE FUN!
PAP!
SEIZE THE DAY! GRAB SUCCESS WITH BOTH HANDS!
I GUESS, IT CAN'T GET MUCH WORSE.
THAT'S THE SPIRIT!

HATS
HATS
PARADISE SPRING
HONESTLY, IT WASN'T MY FAULT THE FISH GOT LOOSE.
YOU COULD LIKE, HEAR ITS BODY SLAPPING AROUND THE APARTMENT.
MY ROOMMATES WERE FREAKING OUT!
THE WERE LIKE "HOW DID THIS HAPPEN AGAIN?" AND "YOU GOTTA MOVE OUT FOR THE SAKE OF MY FISH."
AN ATTITUDE LIKE THAT WON'T HELP ME FIND YOUR FISH!
01
WE NEVER FOUND IT.
REBECCA'S!
OH, WE'RE HERE!
APPARENTLY, WHEN ITS REAL QUIET, YOU CAN STILL HEAR HIM SLAPPING TO THIS DAY.

ALL RIGHT, GAME TIME. I CAN DO THIS.
HIRE ME!
IT'S ALWAYS IMPORTANT TO WASH AND REAPPLY EVERY TWO HOURS.
OTHER STORES WON'T TELL YOU THAT BUT IT'S TRUE!

OH, THERE'S A 90% CHANCE THAT 1 IN 5 OF THOSE EYE SHADOW PALETTES MAY OR MAY NOT CONTAIN ASBESTOS... ALLEGEDLY!
SORRY! JUST LEGAL STUFF, WE HAVE TO TELL EVERY CONSUMER!
MIA!!
WHATEVER.
AIDEN! OH MY GOD, YOU'RE AT MY WORK!!
HECK YEAH, I AM!
YOU'RE WILD! THIS IS WILD!
NEW
WHY ARE YOU HERE? COME TO ACCESSORIZE?
CALM DOWN! CALM DOWN!
WE HAVE MOOD RINGS, BUY 6 GET 4 FREE—WE ALSO HAVE LIMITED EDITION TOE MOOD RINGS!
SALE
MOOD
SALE
SALE!!

NO MOOD RINGS TODAY, MIA. MAYBE LATER THOUGH.
OH! IS THERE AN EMERGENCY WITH THE SHOW?
I KNEW I COULDN'T TRUS THOSE DODGEBALLERS.
THE SHOW'S ALL GOOD FOR NOW! I THINK. MAYBE NOT? MASON'S HANDLING IT.
I'M ACTUALLY HERE TO TALK TO THE MANAGER!
OH, REBECCA? SHE'S OUT FOR THE DAY.
I'M IN CHARGE FOR NOW! SHE'S EVEN LETTING ME BE AN APPRENTICE EAR-PIERCING TECHNICIAN-IN-TRAINING!
WOW! I GUESS I CAN JUST GIVE YOU MY RÉSUMÉ THEN!
WHA—WHAT DO YOU MEAN "RÉSUMÉ?"

MY RÉSUMÉ!
FOR LIKE A JOB!
SALE!!
OH... I DON'T KNOW, AIDEN. ARE YOU SURE YOU'RE A GOOD FIT?
IT'S JUST THAT WE HAVE A REALLY HIGH STANDARD FOR CHEER ADVISORS AT REBECCA'S.
WE REALLY VALUE RESPONSIBILITY, AND BEING ON TIME FOR WORK...
...AND NOT MISPLACING THOUSANDS OF DOLLARS WORTH OF MERCHANDISE, CAUSING THE COMPANY TO GO BANKRUPT LIKE YOUR LAST JOB.
RIGHT.

SORRY DUDE, IF IT WERE UP TO ME, YOU'D AT LEAST BE A GLITTER MONITOR.
IT'S ALRIGHT, I GET IT.
I KNOW I'M NOT THE BEST EMPLOYEE...

OH AIDEN, I'M SORRY...

SIGH

REBECCA'S "X-TREME!!"

I HAVEN'T BEEN TO THIS STORE IN AGES!
DO YOU WANT TO GO IN?
~COOL

I DON'T KNOW. DOESN'T IT FEEL LIKE A BIT MUCH?
SLAM!!

LIKE, DOESN'T THE UNCHECKED CONSUMERISM KIND OF MAKE YOU NAUSEOUS?
SHOW UP EVERYDAY IN EVERY WAY!
LIFE IS GOOD :)
YEAH NOW THAT YOU MENTION IT.
FEELING FREE AND BLESSED EVERY MORNING!
TAKE SELF DOUBT AND THROW IT OUT, QUEEN!
NO! NOT HER! NOT NOW!
WHY ARE WE EVEN AT THE MALL, THEN?
ARTISTIC RESEARCH, OF COURSE.
DOES SHE EVER TAKE A DAY OFF FROM ART?

DO YOU WANT TO GO IN FOR CLOSER RESEARCH?
NAH. STILL WANNA GO TO THE LAST DAY ON EARTH CAFE?
BUMP
?
?
Hmm

HA
HA
HA
HA
Press
CHILL OUT! CHILL OUT!
SWAY
SWAY
WOW. HE REALLY NEEDS MY HELP.
WHAT? WHO?

sway
sway
CRASH!
THUDM
WHY IS EVERYONE I KNOW SO COOL.
CRASH!!
BOOM!!
THUD!!
CRASH!!
BOOM
BANG!!
OH NO! THE LOVELY EARS COLLECTION!

OH NO OH NO OH NO!
ANYTHING THAT TOUCHES THE FLOOR IN THIS STORE IS FINAL SALE! IT'S A BIOHAZARD!
I'M SORRY! I WAS GONNA BUY THOSE ONES, I THINK, BUT MY EARS AREN'T PIERCED—WHOOPS! AH!
XTREME
I'VE GOTTA CALL REBECCA! WE'VE NEVER HAD A PRODUCT LOSS OF THIS SCALE.
I'LL BUY THEM ALL, I SWEAR!
HEY MIA—YOU SAID YOU WERE AN EAR-PIERCING TECHNICIAN, RIGHT?

IN TRAINING...

BEKKIE

THIS IS REBECCA SPARKLE, PLEASE LEAVE A MESSAGE!

10 FREE EARRINGS PER PIERCING!!

IS THAT STILL STORE POLICY?

HECK YEAH, IT IS!

CLICK!

DID YOU FIND SOME EARRINGS YOU LIKED?

THERE WERE SOME BLACK ONES...

YAH!

THEN THAT'S SETTLED.

YOU SAID YOU WANTED TO BE BRAVE!

THIS ISN'T AT ALL WHAT I HAD IN MIND!

THESE THE ONES YOU LIKED?
QUEEN
QUEEN

YOU CAN DO THIS! WHAT BUILDS MORE CONFIDENCE THAN GOING FOR A LOOK YOU ALWAYS WANTED TO TRY?
DOESN'T THIS SEEM EXTREME? I COULD JUST GET CLIP-ONS?!

WHERE'S THE FUN IN THAT?
YOU HAVE TO MAKE SURE YOU DON'T MOVE, I'M STILL WORKING ON MY AIM!
O-OKAY... JUST WARN ME BEFORE YOU DO IT...
ALRIGHT!

3

2

1

IT LOOKSSS SOOOO GOOOOD!

DESPITE ALL THE CRYING, I THINK THEY REALLY SUIT YOU!
PRETZEL PRINCE

SO... BACK
IN REBECCA'S...
DID YOU KNOW THOSE PEOPLE
WHO WERE HANGING OUT
OUTSIDE THE STORE OR..?
UHHH...
SORRY!
NONE OF MY
BUSINESS.
GALE! HANG IN THERE!
DON'T PANIC!

AHHHH!
UM...
SLAM
YOU NEED TO KEEP ICE ON THEM OR THEY'LL GET INFECTED.
W-WHAT? I CAN'T HEAR YOU.

MAKE SURE HE DOESN'T TOUCH HIS EARS FOR A WEEK!
MHM.
WASH WITH SALT WATER EVERY DAY!
RIGHT.

I SHOULDN'T HAVE DONE THIS, MY HUBRIS BLINDED ME!
FLEW TOO CLOSE TO THE FULL-TIME EAR-PIERCING TECHNICIAN SUN?
I'M FINE, I THINK I'M BOUNCING BACK.

YOU BETTER BE!

I COULDN'T HANDLE THE LEGAL REPERCUSSIONS IF YOU DIEEEED!

THERE, THERE. GALE PROMISES NOT TO DIE.
ALIVE AND UH, THRIVING!
WHY DID YOU TALK ME INTO DOING THIS?!
I THOUGHT IT'D BE FUNNY.
I HAVE TO GO BACK, REBECCA'S IS PROBABLY IN CHAOS.
OH, COME ON. WORK'S NOT THAT IMPORTANT. WE'RE GOING TO BEATPLEX EMPORIUM, YOU SHOULD COME!
OH, I DON'T KNOW...
WHAT IF I TOLD YOU HARPER'S WORKING TODAY?
I CAN TAKE A LONG LUNCH!

BZZZ
NEXT STOP, THE LAND OF ETERNAL BEATS!
LET'S GO, LET'S GO, LET'S GO!
REMINDER!
REMEMBER TO DRINK YOUR 12 DAILY CANS OF REFRESHING SIMPLY PEAR!
GALE! LET'S GO!
RIGHT!
!

DO YOU THINK SHE'LL BE FINE WITH US DROPPING IN?
WHAT DO YOU MEAN? I DO IT ALL THE TIME!
HAVE YOU TRIED OUR RESTORATIVE REFRESHERS? BUY SOME TODAY!
GALE, CAN YOU WALK ANY SLOWER?!
!!
CAUSE WE'RE HERE!

THESE WOULD BE AMAZING FOR OUR NEW STAGE VISUALS!
WE'D LOOK SO CUTE PLAYING THESE!
WE'VE BEEN THINKING OF PIVOTING ASTRAL PANIC IN A MORE THEATRICAL DIRECTION.
IT'S BEEN TOUGH GETTING EVERYONE ON BOARD...
...SOME MORE THAN OTHERS.
OH!
IT'D BE SO COOL IF YOU DESIGNED SOME OF OUR OUTFITS!
WHAT? REALLY?
OF COURSE! WE COULD MATCH THE POSTERS! IT'D BE AMAZING!

YOU COULD DESIGN OUR WHOLE EXTENDED UNIVERSE!
IF YOU REALLY THINK SO, I COULD GIVE IT A SHOT.
OF COURSE I THINK SO!
THE VIBE WE'RE GOING FOR IS...
SPACE
JUST LETTING YOU KNOW RIGHT NOW, I'M NOT WEARING ANYTHING I CAN'T BREATHE IN AGAIN.

HARPER!
GALE, THIS IS OUR BASSIST EXTRAORDINAIRE, HARPER.
UH, HI.
HEY.
WHAT BRINGS YOU TWO IN TODAY?
WE WANTED TO SEE YOU!
ARE YOU GUYS HIRING?

WAIT, YOU'RE ACTUALLY LOOKING FOR A NEW JOB?
WHAT HAPPENED TO NEPTUNE'S SEASIDE KITCHEN? I PUT A GOOD WORD IN FOR YOU THERE!
UHHH...
IT WASN'T A GOOD FIT.
RING
RING
RING
DIDN'T YOU SAY THAT ABOUT THE LAST PLACE?

SORRY, I JUST FIGURED SINCE YOU'VE BEEN THROUGH SO MANY JOBS...
...YOU'D HAVE FOUND A GOOD FIT BY NOW.
I'VE HAD A BUNCH OF NOT GOOD FITS.
I JUST HAVE TO FIND THE RIGHT ENVIRONMENT...
I'M WORKING ON IT.
HOW'S THE NEW JOB SEARCH GOING?
REALLY... UH... WELL.
LOTS OF OFFERS!
SEE! HE'LL BE FINE!
ALL FINE!

THAT'S GOOD. IN OTHER NEWS, I ACTUALLY HAVE SOME LESS THAN IDEAL INFORMATION...
SIGH
THE DODGEBALLERS ARE BAILING—THEY'RE NOT COMING TO THE SHOW.
WHAT?!
NO!
CRACK

MASON'S FREAKING OUT.
OH NO...
I BOUGHT A CONFETTI CANNON!
ASTRAL PANIC
WHAT ARE WE GOING TO DO? THAT'S OUR WHOLE AUDIENCE!
THERE'S ALWAYS THE JANITORIAL STAFF.
BZZZ
ENJOY THE MOMENT :)
NOT HELPFUL.

WE'LL FIGURE SOMETHING OUT.

I SHOULD GET BACK TO WORK.

ME TOO.

WE'LL TALK LATER AND COME UP WITH A PLAN.
YEAH, TALK LATER...

JUICE CLEANSE GOING WELL?
ITS MORE LIKE A LIFESTYLE...
SZZZZ
AH!
AND NO, IT'S NOT.

Fizz
IS EVERYTHING GOING TO BE OKAY WITH THE SHOW?
YEAH, OF COURSE! EVERYTHING'S TOTALLY FINE.
I SWEAR! I'M NOT EVEN WORRIED AT ALL!

SO, IS THAT TO HELP WITH EARLIER?
AT REBECCA'S?
SIP
IT WAS JUST SOME PEOPLE FROM MY CLASS, I DON'T REALLY FEEL LIKE TALKING TO THEM RIGHT NOW.
PLAYING IT COOL AND MYSTERIOUS—I GET IT.
MORE LIKE PLAYING IT WEIRD AND STUPID.

I JUST DON'T WANT TO TALK TO PEOPLE WHEN I CAN BARELY GO TO CLASS.
POP!
SKIPPING CLASS? HARDCORE.
EVERYONE'S DOING SO WELL AND EVERY TIME I GO TO CLASS I END UP EMBARRASSING MYSELF.
I THOUGHT YOUR SKELE-WIZARD WAS REALLY COOL!

IT DOESN'T EVEN HOLD A CANDLE TO WHAT OTHER PEOPLE ARE DOING.
SO SCHOOL IS UTTERLY HUMILIATING BECAUSE YOU CAN'T STOP DRAWING WIZARDS?
POP
POP
CRUSH
AMONG OTHER THINGS.
HEY MAN, I SEE TWO SOLUTIONS.

OPTION ONE, YOU CAN STOP DRAWING WIZARDS.
...
THOUGH I DON'T THINK YOU SHOULD DO THAT!
OR TWO...
JUST OWN IT!
IT'S NOT JUST ABOUT WIZARDS, ITS EVERYTHING.
I GET EMBARRASSED OVER THE SMALLEST THING,
HAVE A PANIC ATTACK,
AND FEEL EMBARRASSED ABOUT THE PANIC ATTACK,
TRIGGERING ANOTHER PANIC ATTACK.
ITS LIKE A CYCLE OF PAIN.
I'M SURE NOBODY REALLY NOTICES,
AT LEAST I'M BANKING ON THAT.
PAT PAT

I EMBARRASS MYSELF ALL THE TIME! LIKE, CONSTANTLY! I THINK PEOPLE JUST END UP MOVING ON WITH THEIR LIVES.
IF I BEAT MYSELF UP AFTER EVERY TIME I FELT EMBARRASSED, I WOULD NEVER LEAVE THE HOUSE.
MAYBE THAT'S IT! YOU NEED ONE BIG HUMILIATION TO PROVE IT'S NOT THAT BAD!

SURE... I GUESS.

AFTERNOON RAVE—I FORGOT.
4:30
MAN, I REALLY WISH I COULD WORK HERE.

DO YOU WANNA HEAD HOME?
YEAH.
OH! YOUR SKETCHBOOK!
SORRY.
IT'S OKAY, IT'S BEEN A LONG DAY.
I THINK I JUST NEED TO LIE DOWN.
YEAH ITS GETTING A LITTLE WILD FOR MY TASTE—LET'S HEAD OUT.

THWAK
THWAK
SIGH
EVERYTHING OKAY?
WHAT? YEAH, OF COURSE!
AAALL GOOD.
BESIDES YOU'RE THE ONE WHO HAD A TOUGH DAY.
IT WAS A LOT, BUT I DIDN'T CRACK MY TOP TEN MOST ANXIOUS DAYS. HONESTLY.

HAHA! WELL, THAT'S GOOD AT LEAST.
CLICK
SIGH
HEY, GALE? THANKS FOR COMING OUT WITH ME TODAY.
HONESTLY, I REALLY WASN'T LOOKING FORWARD TO JOB HUNTING AGAIN.

UH...

IF NOT, NO WORRIES!

SURE, SOUNDS FUN.
REALLY?!
THAT'S GOOD, 'CAUSE I HAVE A SURPRISE PLANNED.
OH, GREAT! A SURPRISE...
YOU'RE GONNA LOVE IT!
I PROMISE!
CLAP!!

THANKS!!
Rebecca's!
ASTRAL PANIC
RÉSUMÉ

KNOCK KNOCK
KNOCK KNOCK
LET'S GO, GALE!
INCREDIBLE SURPRISES AWAIT!
BZZZ
BZZZ
GET UP GET UP GET UP!
GOOD MORN—
OH MY!
IS THAT THE FINISHED POSTER?
Y-YEAH I FINISHED IT LAST NIGHT.
WOOOOSHHHH
WOW...
IS IT OKAY?
I DIDN'T KNOW ART COULD BE SO BEAUTIFUL.
01
I HAVE TO SHOW THE OTHERS!

DO YOU THINK THEY'LL LIKE IT?
YES!
BZZZ!!
IS THAT THE POSTER? OUR FIRST REAL POSTER?!
L0$tX!NX $P@¢3 - SENT!
BZZZ!!
NICE.
IT'S MORE THAN JUST NICE!
NICE X 2
BZZZ!!
TAKE A BETTER PICTURE WE NEED TO GET THIS OUT ASAP!
AIDEN! TAKE A BETTER PICTURE!

THEY LOVE IT!
REALLY?
OH, WE NEED TO GO, BRO. INTERVIEW'S IN 15 MINUTES.
12:05
LET'S GO!
01
OH, JUST A SEC.
STOCKING UP?
YOU NEVER KNOW IF YOU'LL NEED IT.

COME ON, HURRY UP! YOUR SURPRISE ISN'T GOING TO WAIT AROUND ALL DAY!
OR MAYBE IT WILL, IT'S HERE ALL WEEK BUT THAT'S NOT THE POINT.
YOU'RE GONNA LOVE IT!
WOOOOSH

SUNNY SIDE BEACH
NO SWIMMING
OKIE DOKIE, HERE WE GO!
ONLY ONCE IN A MILLENNIA WILL YOUR DEEPEST PASSION COME TO FRUITION LIKE THIS, GALE...

TA-DA!
UH... BUCCANEER BASH?

YOU CAN USE THIS AS INSPIRATION FOR YOUR NEXT MASTERPIECE.
IT'S NOT EXACTLY SKELE-WIZARD, BUT THEY'RE IN THE SAME REALM.
ARE THEY?
THEY DEFINITELY ARE. NOW, HURRY UP!
HUFF HUFF
HURRY UP! HURRY UP! HURRY UP!

YOU CAN ENJOY THE AMBIENCE WHILE I'M IN MY INTERVIEW.

YOU'LL HAVE A GOOD TIME, I PROMISE!

GALE!
OVER
HERE!
CHECK OUT
THESE DUDES!
THE GUY SAID TO
MEET HIM BY THE
ART INSTALLATION—
DOES THIS LOOK
LIKE ART?
WHATEVER, AFTER TODAY YOU'RE
GOING TO BE IN THE PRESENCE OF
A PROFESSIONAL WORKING MA—
GET OFF
THE STATUE!!!

DON'T TOUCH THE ART!
STOP TOUCHING THE ART!
GET OFF!
GET OFF!
GET OFF!
THESE PIECES ARE PRICELESS! WHAT ARE YOU THINKING?!
SORRY...
SORRY!
KIDS THESE DAYS. NO RESPECT FOR THE ARTS!

MÉ!!
A+!!
#1
YOU'RE NOT HERE FOR THE INTERVIEW ARE YOU?
I AM!
I NEED TO VET RÉSUMÉS BETTER.
ALRIGHT KID, WE'RE ON STRIKE ONE—I'VE GOT MY EYE ON YOU.

COME ON, FOLLOW ME.
YESSIR!
I'LL BE BACK SOON. DON'T HAVE TOO MUCH FUN WHILE I'M GONE!
HURRY UP! YOU'RE WASTING DAYLIGHT, KID!
YESSIR!

!!
HAHA
HA
HA

OH MY GOD, I KNOOOW RIGHT?

HA
HA

HA
HA
HAHA
HAHA
HA
HA
HA
HA
HA
HA
HA
HA

SAVE MY BEAUTIFUL MANSION!
!!
TAP
TAP
TAP

ALRIGHT.
A—
ARDEN..?
Ard
•Hard worker, obviously
100%
3 A(+) words to describe me:
•AGILE
WE'RE LOOKING FOR SERIOUS CANDIDATES ONLY FOR THE CRYSTAL CLEAR BEACH WATER MAINTENANCE AND SURVEILLANCE POSITION.
YOU CAN COUNT ON ME, SIR!
WELL, YOU'RE NOT OFF TO A GOOD START, SO I'LL BE THE JUDGE OF THAT.

THE AYE AYE MATEY FESTIVAL IS GOING TO BE HERE ALL WEEK.
WE NEED THIS WATER IN TIP-TOP SHAPE.
YES, SIR!
ALRIGHT, COOL IT.
I'M SURE YOU'VE SEEN THE SIGNS. THE WATER'S NOT ALWAYS THE, ERM... HEALTHIEST. IT NEEDS FREQUENT TESTING AND SURVEILLANCE.
NO SWIMMING!!
No Swim!
AND THAT'S WHERE YOU COME IN.

HA
HAHA
WOOOOOOOOOW
HAH
HA
HA
HA
HAHAHAHAHA
HAHAHAHA
HA
HA
HA
HA
HA
HA
HA
HA
HAHAHA
HA
HA
HAHAHA
HAHAHAHAHA
MY MANSION!
HAHAHA!
WHATEVER!

OUCH!
!!

HAHAHAHAHA HA
HAH
HA HAHAHA
HAHA HAHA
HAHAHA
HAHAHA
HAHAHA
Ding
Simply Reminder!
GAME OVER
FEELING A LITTLE STRESSED, GALE?
ONE DAY OUT WON'T SOLVE ALL YOUR PROBLEMS! THERE'S STILL SO MUCH MORE YOU CAN DO!

YOU'RE GETTING STRESSED OUT JUST STANDING HERE!
STANDING ALONE ISN'T THAT HARD! TRY TALKING TO SOMEONE THAT MIGHT HELP!
YESTERDAY PUSHED YOU OUT OF YOUR COMFORT ZONE BUT COULD YOU DO MORE?
WANT MORE RELAXING PEAR JUICE? CLICK HERE TO ORDER MORE!
JUST BREATHE, JUST BREATHE. NOTHING'S EVEN HAPPENING.

ARDEN! GET OVER HERE AND LOOK AT THIS!
YESSIR!

NOW YOU CAN'T TELL JUST BY LOOKING AT IT, BUT THIS WATER'S NOT SAFE FOR SWIMMING TODAY.

IT NEEDS TO BE TESTED.

THIS JOB IS LIFE-AND-DEATH, DO YOU UNDERSTAND?
I UNDERSTAND, SIR!

I'M FINE, I CAN DO THIS. I'M JUST WAITING FOR AIDEN TO GET BACK.
YOU DON'T SEEM FINE, GALE.
I AM FINE.
REALLY? YOU SEEM LIKE YOU'RE ABOUT TO PANIC.
KEEP CALM, GALE.
EVERYONE'S STARING AT YOU, GALE.
BETTER STOP PANICKING.

COME ON, GALE, STOP PANICKING.
YOU'RE EMBARRASSING YOURSELF.
SWAY SWAY
Bzzzz
Bzzzz
Bzzzz
Bzzzz
BUMP
GALE!
STOP PANICKING, GALE!
BUMP!
GALE!
GALE!
GALE!

WATCH CLOSELY, KID, YOUR LIFE DEPENDS ON IT.
I'M WATCHING, SIR.
ONE.
YOU TAKE YOUR ARM...
...STICK IT IN THE WATER.
HOLD FOR 30 SECONDS.
THEN, OUT OF THE WATER.
NOW, YOU WAIT 70 SECONDS.

IF YOU START NOTICING REDNESS... ITCHING...
DON'T
NO Swimming!
PUT OUT THE NO SWIM SIGN FOR THE DAY.
SKIN HEALTHY AND BUMP-FREE? YOU'RE CLEAR.
FOR NOW.
THAT'S... THE JOB?

I'M FINE.
I'M FINE.
I'M FINE!

BLOOP!

INVITE!!
MOM'S BIRTHDAY

SIMPLY REMINDER!

ASSIGNMENT OVER DUE!!!

ASTRAL PANIC

7:30 @ CHARLE'S FUN EMPORIUM!!
PLZ COME!!!!!

GALE!
COME ON, GALE.
OH GALE, YOU REALLY ARE FAILING ON ALL FRONTS.
BZZZ
BZZZ
BZZZ
BZZZ
BZZZ BZZZ
BZZZ!!
YOU SHOULD JUST GO HOME BEFORE YOU EMBARRASS YOURSELF MORE.
BUMP
HAHA
HA
HAHA

!!
CRASH
BOOM
BANG

THIS JOB IS EASY!
NOT EASY! LIFE-AND-DEATH KID!
ALRIGHT, I GUESS YOU'RE READY FOR THE INTERVIEW PORTION.
I THOUGHT... THAT WAS THE INTERVIEW...
BANG
CRASH
BANG
WHAT THE—?!

CRASH
BANG
CRACK

BANG
CRASH!!
CRACK!

HEY! WHAT DO YOU THINK YOU'RE DOING?!
THE SCULPTURES, THE FESTIVAL!

THE ART!
GALE!
RUN!
HAHAHA!
GET BACK HERE!
YOU'RE GONNA
PAY FOR THIS!

HUFF
HUFF

GRAB

AHHHHHHHH

WELL,
THAT WASN'T SO BAD!
OH! I GOT SOMETHING FOR YOU! SOMETHING TO REMEMBER THE DAY BY!
UM!!
VOILA!
LIFE'S A BEACH!

NOW WHEN YOU'RE STRESSED, YOU CAN JUST REMEMBER THAT LIFE'S A BEACH! AND ALL THAT.
BESIDES, I WOULDN'T WORRY TOO MUCH ABOUT THAT TOXIC BEACH, ANYWAYS. YOU'RE LIKE A HERO OR SOMETHING, CLEANING THAT PLACE OUT.
I THOUGHT THAT APPLYING FOR JOBS WOULD BE BORING, BUT YOU'RE BRINGING THE PARTY.
OPEN

HAHAHA! STOP IT!
HA HA
HA HA
HA
HA
HA
JUST A SEC, I GOTTA GET MY WALLET.
IS EVERYTHING OKAY?
?

NO, NO, NO.
NOT NOW!

DO YOU KNOW THOSE GUYS?

BRIBED HER WAY INTO THE POTTERY STUDIO. DOES ALL HER PROJECTS ON HAND-THROWN FLOWER VASES.
TOP OF THE CLASS, BELOVED BY ALL.
3D-PRINTED ALL THE TEACHERS' CHRISTMAS GIFTS AND IS NOW IN THE A+ POCKET FOR LIFE.
I... I HAVE TO GO... I CAN'T DO THIS RIGHT NOW.

GALE?!
GALE!
WAIT UP!

HUFF
HUFF
HUFF

SLAM!!

SLAM!!
WELCOME TO—

WHATEVER.

RESTROOM
BANG
GASP!
SLAM!

HUFF
HUFF
WELCOME—
SLAM
HRMMM.
!!
GALE?
$
!!
Roll

CLACK
CLACK
CLACK
GASP
GASP
GASP
GASP
HEYYY BUDDY,
YOU DOING OKAY?
NO.
I'M HERE IF YOU
WANNA TALK.
IT'S NOT WORKING.
NONE OF IT IS WORKING.
DRIP
DRIP

I'M STILL PANICKING ALL THE TIME! I DON'T HAVE THE COURAGE OF TEN THOUSAND LIONS THAT SHINE AS BRIGHT AS THE MORNING SUN!
#1!
WOW, THOSE ADS DO PROMISE A LOT.
I DON'T WANT TO FEEL LIKE THIS ANY MORE.
THIS STUFF IS SUPPOSED TO HELP.
NO MATTER WHAT I DO, I STILL FEEL ANXIOUS AND EVERYTHING'S GOING HORRIBLY.

YOU STILL DID IT, THOUGH.
...I JUST DESTROYED A WHOLE FESTIVAL AND PRICELESS WORKS OF ART.
#1!
PRICELESS? THEY WERE COVERED IN BIRD POOP! HOW PRICELESS COULD THEY BE?
YEAH, YOU DESTROYED THEM! AND IT DOESN'T MATTER!
YOU'RE NOT GOING TO GET ME TO SEE TODAY AS A WIN.
#1!

MAYBE IT IS A WIN.
IT'S NOT A WIN!
YOU DID EVERYTHING YOU WANTED TO DO THOUGH, EVEN THOUGH YOU WERE ANXIOUS!
YOU HUNG OUT WITH ME ALL DAY YESTERDAY AND CAME OUT TODAY. THAT'S GOTTA COUNT FOR SOMETHING!
I JUST HAD A PANIC ATTACK.
I DON'T THINK THAT'S A FAILURE.

BESIDES, YOU DID IT WITH STYLE! YOU REALLY DREW A CROWD!

AND NOW LOOK AT YOU! YOU'RE STILL STANDING! YOU SURVIVED IT!

BZZZZZZ

YOU'RE CRUSHING IT, GALE! YOU'RE REALLY DOING IT!
ANXIETY CAN GET IN THE WAY OF SUCCESS!
CALM DOWN WITH A SOOTHING SIMPLY PEAR DRINK!

EVEN THOUGH YOU'RE SCARED!
YOU'RE AMAZING!
DON'T STRIVE FOR HALF SUCCESSES!
YOU'VE RANKED AS MORE ANXIOUS THAN 95% OF SOCIETY! SOMETIMES YOU JUST NEED TO WORK A BIT HARDER!

THIS JOB SEARCH HASN'T BEEN GOING SO WELL FOR ME. I'VE MESSED UP, UH, A LOT OF OPPORTUNITIES BEFORE...

...BUT, I DON'T KNOW, IF YOU CAN KEEP GOING AFTER A COUPLE CASES OF PROPERTY DAMAGE, MAYBE I CAN TOO...
...A LOT OF THIS PROBABLY SUCKS BUT MAYBE IT'LL BE WORTH IT IN THE END.
LIFES A BEACH!
BESIDES, THOSE PIRATE HEADS WILL GET OVER IT IN NO TIME!

PIRATES ARE GOOD AT BUILDING STUFF, RIGHT?
I GUESS THEY COULD BE.
THEY'LL HAVE IT FIXED IN NO TIME!
AIDEN?
YEAH?
LiFE'S
I HAVEN'T DONE EVERYTHING I WANTED TO DO.
OH?
?
PSSSSST!
THERE'S STILL YOUR SHOW, I FINISHED THE POSTER AND EVERYTHING.
IF YOU WANT TO COME, THERE'S STILL TIME!
I... I DON'T KNOW.
IT COULDN'T BE ANY WORSE THAN WHAT JUST HAPPENED TEN MINUTES AGO!

YOU FLATTENED A WHOLE FESTIVAL!
AND YOU RAN SO FAST! YOU'LL NEVER GET CAUGHT!
THE WORST HAS HAPPENED AND YOU DEFEATED IT.
YOU CAN DO ANYTHING! YOU'RE ON TOP OF THE WORLD!
YOU THINK..?

YOU'RE ALREADY DOING IT!
YOU'RE LIKE A GOD!
ALRIGHT, THAT'S ENOUGH.
BZZZZZZ
BE CAREFUL NOT TO MAKE THINGS WORSE!
POWER OFF!! :)

IT'S NOT GOING TO BE THAT BAD?
FOR YOU, NO WAY! YOU'RE A MACHINE, AN ANXIOUS LITTLE MACHINE! IF SOMETHING DOES GO WRONG, IT'LL PROBABLY JUST MAKE THE SHOW BETTER.
KICK
YOU REALLY THINK I CAN DO IT?

WITH EVERY FIBER
OF MY BEING!

GRIP

ALRIGHT... I'LL GO!
I'LL GO TO THE SHOW!
YES!!!

YOU'RE MY HERO, GALE!

PFFFFt!!

CAN YOU KEEP IT DOWN?! THIS IS A FAST DINING ESTABLISHMENT! IF YOU WANT TO PLAY THERAPIST, TAKE IT OUTSIDE!

SLAM!
WELL, THAT'S GONNA BE ANOTHER FAILED INTERVIEW.
YOU HAVE AN INTERVIEW HERE TOO?!
I'M SORRY FOR RUINING YOUR BEACH MONITOR OPPORTUNITY THING...
EH, IT'S FINE. I PROBABLY WASN'T GOING TO GET IT ANYWAY.
YOU DON'T KNOW THAT!
IT'S FINE, USUALLY I'M THE ONE MESSING UP MY INTERVIEWS.
I SHOULD THANK YOU. NOW I HAVE SOMEONE ELSE TO BLAME WHEN I GET TURNED DOWN!
YEAH, NO PROBLEM...

YOU SURE IT'S OKAY?
IT'S FINE GALE! ANOTHER DAY, ANOTHER OPPORTUNITY. WE'RE GOOD.
THE GUILT IS STARTING TO SET IN.
STOP IT! I'M JUST GLAD WE'LL HAVE AT LEAST ONE AUDIENCE MEMBER FOR THE SHOW.
B-BUT...
JUST GO HOME, BUD. YOU LOOK EXHAUSTED.
YEAH, OKAY.
MAKE SURE TO AVOID THE BEACH, THEY'RE PROBABLY STILL LOOKING FOR YOU.
R-RIGHT.

DAY OF THE SHOW!!
DON'T BE FOOLED BY APPEARANCES, THIS PLACE IS SUPER EXCLUSIVE. WE GET FIRST PICK OF THE PRIZE COUNTS AND EVERYTHING.
?
WOW!
ASTRAL PANIC
ASTRAL PANIC
MY-MY POSTER!
IT LOOKS AMAZING!
01

WE'VE BEEN PUTTING THEM UP EVERYWHERE. I CAN'T BELIEVE IT WORKED!
GRAB ONE FOR ME TOO!
NOW, HOPEFULLY THEY LIKE THE MUSIC JUST AS MUCH...
YOU READY TO DO THIS?
MHM.
EVEN THE DODGE BALLERS ARE HERE! GALE, YOU'RE A GENIUS!

HOW'S IT GOING?

I'D RATHER BE PLAYING TO AN EMPTY ROOM.

OH. I HAVE SOME TOKENS I WANT TO TRADE IN.

DON'T BOTHER, I ALREADY TRIED.

HE'S CLOSING THE COUNTER EARL BECAUSE SERVING THE CUSTOMERS IS "SAFETY HAZARD."

THEY KEEP THROWING THE PRIZES AT MY HEAD.

I BET THEY'RE ACCURATE, TOO.
THEY HAVEN'T MISSED YET.
DON'T YOU HAVE A DUMB COSTUME TO CHANGE INTO? MIA'S BEEN BACKSTAGE WAITING FOR YOU.
RIGHT!
GALE, THERE'S A SEAT THERE FOR YOU.
WOOSH!
WOOSH!
PERFECT FOR OUR GUEST OF HONOR!
PING!
SQUEAK
ALRIGHT GALE, THIS IS THE MOMENT OF TRUTH!
I WON'T BE HERE TO PROTECT YOU FOREVER. SIT HERE, WATCH THE SHOW AND HAVE FUN.
IF YOU FEEL LIKE YOU'RE GONNA PUKE, I GIVE YOU FULL PERMISSION TO PUKE ON MASON'S STUFF.
IF YOU PUKE ON THE FLOOR, IT COMES OUT OF OUR TOKEN PAYMENT.
SPIN!

I'M SO PROUD
OF YOU.
WE GOTTA GO.
HAVE FUN AND
STAY SAFE!
DON'T DO ANYTHING
I WOULDN'T DO. I KNOW
YOU LIKE TO GET WILD!
WE NEED
TO GO!
SIGH

BZZZ
BZZZ
BZZZ
BZZZ
BZZZ
BZZZ
BZZZ

woooo!
woo!
BZZZ
BZZZ
STRUM
BZZZ
BZZZ
BZZZ

HOPE YOU'RE HAVING A GOOD TIME ON THIS FINE WEDNESDAY AFTERNOON!
I KNOW EVERYONE'S DISAPPOINTED THAT THE PRIZE COUNTER'S CLOSED, BUT WE CAN STILL PARTY ANYWAYS!
WOO!!
BEFORE WE START, WE NEED TO REITERATE—NO CLIMBING ON CHARLES!
BOO!
THIS SONG IS CALLED "IT'S HARD TO SING WITH THIS MASK ON AND I APOLOGIZE IN ADVANCE!"
WE WROTE IT THIS MORNING!
THANK YOU VERY MUCH, WE'RE ASTRAL PANIC!

THREE!
TWO!
ONE!
LET'S GO!
BZZZ
BZZZ
BZZZ
BZZZ

HOW'S IT GOING, GALE?

ISN'T IT HARD TO RELAX WHEN EVERYONE'S STARING AT YOU?
SITTING ALLLLL ALONE.
WE SHOULD JUST GO HOME.
EVERYONE THINKS YOU'RE WEIRD HERE, ANYWAY.
THIS THING IS ITCHY!
ITCHY!
JUST ONE MORE SONG. I CAN DO THIS.

LEAVE!
LEAVE! LEAVE!
RUN!
YOU HAVE TO LEAVE!
GET OUT OF HERE!
ARE YOU EVEN LISTENING?
LIFE'S A BEACH!
WE HAVE TO GET OUT OF HERE. YOU'RE GONNA PANIC AND RUIN EVERYTHING!

I'M STAYING FOR ONE SONG, I CAN AT LEAST DO THAT.
WE HAVE TO GET OUT OF HERE!
YOU'RE GONNA PANIC SOON!
THIS NEXT ONE GOES OUT TO MY NEW FRIEND, GALE—IF HE IS STILL HERE TO HEAR IT!
IT'S CALLED, "THE DESTROYER: ARTS AND CULTURE BEWARE! PART TWO!"
CLAP CLAP
OKAY, I GUESS I HAVE TO STAY FOR THIS ONE TOO.

GALE!
ARE YOU EVEN LISTENING?!
GALE!
GALE!
PAY ATTENTION!

STOP HAVING A GOOD TIME!

THAT'S SO UNFAIR!
I'M JUST SAYING, HIS CHARACTER HAS A REDEMPTION ARC!
IN THE LAST ACT!
HE SHOULDN'T HAVE TURNED INTO A GIANT CANNON TO BEGIN WITH!
PRINCESS KNIFE NEEDED TO FORGIVE HIM! IT'S ABOUT FRIENDSHIP!
YEAH AND UP UNTIL THAT POINT HE ACTED LIKE A JERK AND REPEATEDLY—
WELL...
REPEATEDLY—
OH MAN, I CAN'T WAIT TO BE AS COOL AS YOU TWO SOMEDAY.
MUNCH MUNCH!!
YOU RECOVERING YOUR STRENGTH?
MMHMM.
CRUNCH
CRUNCH

I CAN'T BELIEVE YOU STAYED FOR THE WHOLE SHOW!
I KNEW YOU COULD DO IT.
LIFE'S A BEACH!
OH, YOU DO LIKE IT!
MAN, YOU'RE JUST WILD ABOUT PIRATES.
YEAH... I GUESS.

AIDEN, YOU AGREE WITH ME, RIGHT?
HE IS A HUGE JERK. BUT IN LIKE, AN ENDEARING WAY?
BZZZ
BZZZ
SIMPLY REMINDER
SIMPLY REMINDER
SIMPLY REMINDER
SIMPLY REMINDER
BZZZ
SURE, HE TURNED ON HIS WHOLE VILLAGE AND BETRAYED HIS FRIENDS...
...BUT IN A COOL WAY.
BZZZ!!
REMINDER!!

YOU AGREE WITH ME, RIGHT, GALE?

HE DOES HAVE THE COOLEST ULTIMATE ATTACKS.

GALE AGREES WITH ME!
I DON'T TRUST ANY OF YOUR OPINIONS!
HA HA HA
HA HA HA
I'M RIGHT ALL THE TIME ABOUT EVERYTHING!
STOP YELLING!
NO!
HA HA

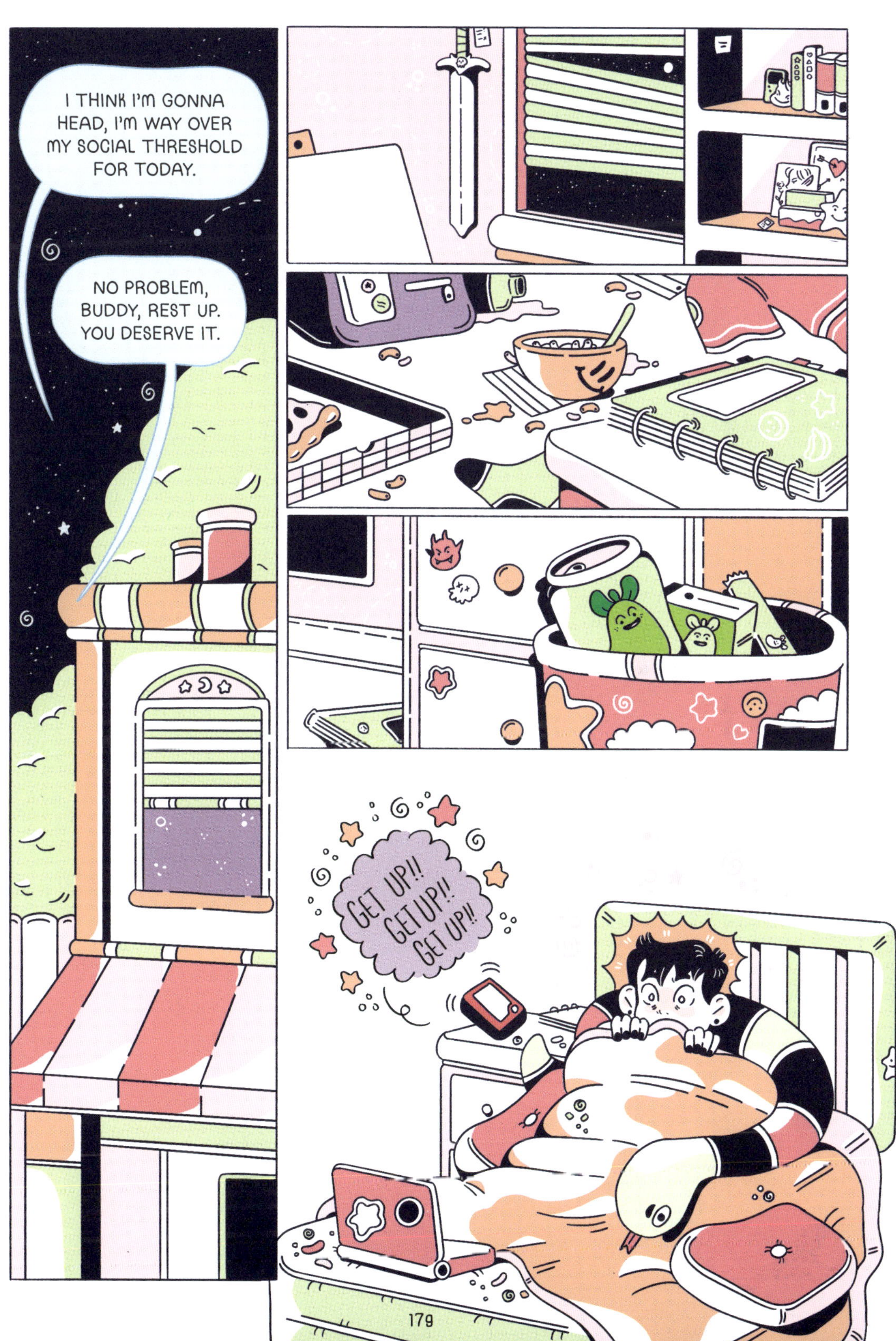
I THINK I'M GONNA HEAD, I'M WAY OVER MY SOCIAL THRESHOLD FOR TODAY.
NO PROBLEM, BUDDY, REST UP. YOU DESERVE IT.
GET UP!! GET UP!! GET UP!!

ALRIGHT, LET'S DO THIS!
2001
LET'S GO!

GALE! OVER HERE! HIYA!
OKAY, LET'S GO.

!
?
OH, GALE! YOU SCARED ME.
SORRY!
I'M JUST HELPING MS. UMBER FOR THE DAY.
OH, THAT'S COOL.
I SAW YOU AT THE BEACH THE OTHER DAY. I WANTED TO SAY HI, BUT YOU SEEMED LIKE YOU WERE IN A HURRY.
YEAH, SORRY. THAT WAS A BUSY DAY FOR ME.
I HEAR YA.
HANDING THAT IN?

YEAH, LATE ASSIGNMENT.
OOOOH!
O-OKAY, I'M GONNA GO—
ASTRAL PANIC
THIS IS COOL! IT'S JUST LIKE THE WIZARDS AND WARLOCKS CAMPAIGN I JUST DID!
R-REALLY?
YEAH! WIZARD SKELETON AND EVERYTHING!
TAP TAP TAP
YOU SHOULD JOIN OUR NEXT CAMPAIGN, I'M TEXTING YOU THE DETAILS RIGHT NOW...
ALRIGHT, GOT TO GO! SEE YA LATER, GALE!
OH, OKAY. THANKS!
B-BYE!
LATERS!

I HANDED IN MY ASSIGNMENT.
CLICK
I DID IT!
BZZZ
BZZZ
AIDEN
HELLO..?
GUESS WHO GOT THE JOB!
WHAT JOB?
SAY HELLO TO THE NEW HEAD OF DEBRIS AND WASTE MANAGEMENT AT CRYSTAL CLEAR BEACH!

APPARENTLY, YOU CAUSED SO MUCH DAMAGE TO THE FESTIVAL THAT THEY WERE JUST DYING TO HIRE ME TO HELP CLEAN UP.
IT'S MANDATORY AND UNPAID FOR NOW, BUT ONCE I GET MY FOOT IN THE DOOR, I'LL BE MOVING MY WAY UP TO WATER TESTING IN NO TIME!
YOU JUST WAIT AND SEE, THEY'RE GOING TO LOVE ME.
ASSIGNMENT HAS MADE TOUCHDOWN OR—UH WHATEVER.
GALE! THAT'S AMAZING DUDE! OH, I HAVE ANOTHER SURPRISE...
I NOMINATED YOU TO PAINT THE NEW PIRATE SCULPTURES AT THE FESTIVAL! COOL, RIGHT?
OH. WOW, THANKS.
NO PROBLEM!
HEY, WE SHOULD GO TO CHARLES' TONIGHT TO CELEBRATE!
I'VE GOT SOME TOKENS SAVED UP AND I WANNA BLOW THEM ALL ON STICKY HANDS AND GUM!

DO YOU WANT TO COME ALONG? I'M GOING TO TRY TO SEE HOW MANY HANDS I CAN STICK TO MASON BEFORE HE NOTICES AND I NEED SOMEONE TO DISTRACT HIM.

YEAH SURE—SOUNDS FUN.
THAT'S WHAT I'M TALKING ABOUT!

KATIE HICKS IS AN ILLUSTRATOR AND COMIC ARTIST LIVING IN THE GREATER TORONTO AREA WITH THEIR PARTNER AND CAT. UP UNTIL THIS POINT, THEY HAVE BEEN SELF-PUBLISHING COMICS AS WELL AS DOING ILLUSTRATION WORK. THEY RECEIVED THEIR BA IN ILLUSTRATION FROM SHERIDAN COLLEGE AND USED THAT KNOWLEDGE TO MAKE THIS COMIC.

EXPLORE MORE
YA TITLES FROM
FLYING EYE BOOKS
JOHN MOORE
NEETOLS
DITCHING SASKIA
FLYING EYE BOOKS
LUCIE BRYON
THIEVES
"Complex, flawed characters that you can't help but love."
– ALICE OSEMAN, HEARTSTOPPER
FLYING EYE BOOKS
TYRELL WAITERS
VERN CUSTODIAN OF THE UNIVERSE
FLYING EYE BOOKS
FLYINGEYEBOOKS.COM

First edition published in 2025 by Flying Eye Books Ltd.
27 Westgate Street, London, E8 3RL.
www.flyingeyebooks.com

Represented by: Authorised Rep Compliance Ltd. Ground Floor,
71 Lower Baggot Street, Dublin, D02 P593, Ireland.
www.arccompliance.com

Edited by Niamh Jones
Designed by Eloise Grohs

1 3 5 7 9 10 8 6 4 2

ISBN: 978-1-83874-208-9
US Library ISBN: 978-1-83874-939-2

Published in the US by Flying Eye Books Ltd.
Printed in China on FSC® certified paper.

ASTRAL
PANIC